The Tiara Club

Midnight Masquerade

For Princess Samantha,
and her dad, King George
VF
With special thanks to JD

www.tiaraclub.co.uk

ORCHARD BOOKS
338 Euston Road, London NW1 3BH
Orchard Books Australia
Level 17/207 Kent St, Sydney, NSW 2000

A Paperback Original
First published in Great Britain in 2008
Text copyright © Vivian French 2008
Cover illustration copyright © Sarah Gibb 2008
Inside illustration copyright © Orchard Books 2008

A CIP catalogue record for this book is available
from the British Library.

ISBN 978 1 84616 882 6

1 3 5 7 9 10 8 6 4 2

Printed in Great Britain

Orchard Books is a division of Hachette Children's Books,
an Hachette Livre UK company

www.hachettelivre.co.uk

The Tiara Club

Midnight Masquerade

With Princess Emma & Princess Jasmine

By Vivian French

ORCHARD BOOKS

The Royal Palace Academy
for the Preparation of Perfect Princesses

(Known to our students as "*The Princess Academy*")

OUR SCHOOL MOTTO:
*A Perfect Princess always thinks of others
before herself, and is kind, caring and truthful.*

Emerald Castle offers a complete education for Tiara Club princesses while taking full advantage of our seaside situation. The curriculum includes:

*A visit to Emerald Sea
World Aquarium and
Education Pool*

*Swimming lessons
(safely supervised at
all times)*

A visit to Seabird Island

Whale watching

Our headteacher, Queen Gwendoline, is present at all times, and students are well looked after by the school Fairy Godmother, Fairy Angora.

Our resident staff and visiting experts include:

*QUEEN MOLLY
(Sports and games)*

*KING JONATHAN
(Captain of the Royal Yacht)*

*LORD HENRY
(Natural History)*

*QUEEN MOTHER MATILDA
(Etiquette, Posture and
Flower Arranging)*

We award tiara points to encourage our Tiara Club princesses towards the next level. All princesses who win enough points at Emerald Castle will be presented with their Emerald Sashes and attend a celebration ball.

Emerald Sash Tiara Club princesses are invited to return to Diamond Turrets, our superb residence for Perfect Princesses, where they may continue their education at a higher level.

PLEASE NOTE:
Princesses are expected to arrive at the Academy with a *minimum* of:

TWENTY BALLGOWNS
(with all necessary hoops, petticoats, etc)

TWELVE DAY DRESSES

SEVEN GOWNS
suitable for parties and other special day occasions

TWELVE TIARAS

DANCING SHOES
five pairs

VELVET SLIPPERS
three pairs

RIDING BOOTS
two pairs

Cloaks, ice skates, winter boots, gloves and other essential outdoor accessories as required

Hello...this is Princess Emma.
I'm so very, VERY glad you're here,
because I've never been to a boarding
school before....have you? I'd read a lot
of books about it, and it sounded
fun - but only if you have loads and
loads of friends. And before I went to
the Princess Academy I didn't
have many friends...

Chapter One

When my mother and father announced that they were going on an extra long Royal Tour, I was thrilled. I've always gone with them, ever since I was tiny – and it's fun! Of course you have to do lots of waving at people, and smile until your cheeks are REALLY sore – but I've never minded doing that.

Does that make me sound like a show-off? I never thought of it that way. It was just something I did because my mum and dad told me to...and (here's the secret bit I don't tell most people) it meant I could stay with them, instead of having to stay at home. I HATE being at home without them. (You won't tell anyone, will you?) So when Mum said something about staying with Aunt Alice for part of the Royal Tour I said, "Ooooh! That'll be fun!"

And then it happened. Mum gave me a surprised look and said, "Oh, Emma! Didn't your father tell you?

You're not coming with us this time. You're going to go to school!"

I burst into tears, even though we were just outside the stables, and the stable boy was looking at me. I SO didn't want to be sent away!

Oh dear. You'll think I'm a terrible baby – but I promised myself I'd tell the truth, because a Perfect Princess always does.

Anyway, I began to cry, and Mum gave me a hug. She said she was really sorry – Dad was supposed to have told me the day before.

"I don't have to go, do I?" I sniffed. "I want to go with you and Dad, like always."

Mum shook her head. "I'm sorry, darling. It's all arranged. The Princess Academy is where I went when I was your age, and I LOVED it." A wistful look came over her face. "It was the happiest time of my life. I made SO many friends while I was there, and you will, too."

I didn't think she was right, but I couldn't say so. If I'd said anything else I'd have started crying again, and the stable boy was still staring at me. Even my pony, Bubbles, was giving me a disapproving look.

Mum took my hand. "Come along," she said. "I've got all the details in my office. I'll show you the school prospectus – and there's also a letter from my dear friend, Queen Tallulah. Her daughter's going to the Academy tomorrow as well, and we've arranged for the two of you to travel together. Isn't that lovely? You'll arrive with a friend, so you'll be just fine!"

I hardly heard what Mum was saying about friends. I'd heard the word *tomorrow* – and I could hardly breathe.

"T...T...TOMORROW?" I gasped.
"I've got to go TOMORROW?"

Mum nodded. "Didn't I say? Mrs Stacey's up in your room now, packing your trunk. SUCH a good thing we bought you those new ballgowns! You'll look SO sweet at the Midnight Masquerade."

"What Midnight Masquerade?" I was beginning to wonder if I was fast asleep and having a horrible nightmare.

"There's always a ball during the Christmas term," Mum told me. "And this year it's extra special. The princes from the Princes' Academy will be there, and you'll all be wearing masks until midnight." And she actually

did a little spin in the middle
of the stable yard! The little
stable boy's eyes opened VERY
wide, and Bubbles whinnied
in surprise.

Before I could say anything else Mum hurried me away to our palace...and I felt more and MORE as if it was all a terrible dream.

Chapter Two

The next twenty-four hours were an absolute whirl. Mrs Stacey, our housekeeper, packed a huge trunk of clothes for me, and Mum told me so many things about school I couldn't remember half of them. She said I was going to be staying somewhere called Emerald Castle, and it was by the sea.

I was to look out for the school fairy godmother, Fairy G, who was lovely. Then she went on and ON about deportment classes and magical islands and sandy beaches until my head was so muddled I burst into floods of tears.

"I don't want to go!" I wailed... but it was no good. Mum told me to be a Perfect Princess, and Dad gave me a big hug and said I was to be a good girl. And the next thing I knew I was in our massive travelling coach.

We rattled along the roads until we got to the weirdest castle I ever saw – all tall turrets and tiny windows – and this strange girl climbed into the coach beside me. She didn't look like any other princess I'd ever seen; she had short spiky hair, and she was dressed in the oddest clothes. She also looked very cross.

"Hello," she said gruffly. "I'm Jasmine. Do you want to go to school?"

I shook my head, and she leant towards me. "Nor do I. Not one bit. I told Ma, but she wouldn't listen. She said school had been the happiest time of her life, and I'd make loads of friends."

"That's EXACTLY what my mum said!" I stared at Jasmine in surprise, and she smiled back. Her whole face lit up, and she looked SO different.

"My mum was at the Princess Academy," I told her, "and she kept telling me about fairy godmothers and masked balls. It sounds weird."

Jasmine giggled. "Bet all the princesses are weird too. Hey – why don't we make a pact? We'll stick together, and we won't be friends with anyone else – well, not unless they're REALLY nice."

"OK," I said, and we shook hands on it.

After that we couldn't stop talking, and it seemed no time at all until the coachman announced, "Emerald Castle, Your Highnesses!"

"WOW!" Jasmine looked out of the window. "I didn't know it was by the sea. This might be better than we thought!"

I didn't want to admit it, but I was feeling the exact opposite. The castle looked enormous, and I felt terribly homesick. And there was the strangest looking fairy standing on the doorstep waiting to greet us; she was wearing BOOTS! I heard Jasmine giggle, but before either of us could say a word the fairy strode towards us.

"Emma and Jasmine, I presume!" she boomed, and her voice was SO loud. "I'm Fairy G, and I'm here to take you to your dormitory. We're putting you in Daffodil Room; you should both enjoy yourselves there. Nice group of girls." She stopped, and winked at me. "Are you Veronica's girl?"

"Er...yes," I said, and I did SO hope she didn't notice my voice was shaking.

"H'mph!" Fairy G's eyes began to twinkle. "Well, I hope you're tidier than she was! She had more minus tiara points for being untidy than any other princess."

"I'm so sorry...are you sure you mean my mother?" I couldn't believe what Fairy G had just said, but she began to laugh.

"I don't suppose she's told you half the things she did," she chortled. "But never mind that now. Let's get you settled, and then you can meet the other princesses over tea. I hope you've got warm gloves with you – tomorrow we've got the Snow Sculpture Competition."

My mouth dropped open. SNOW? What was she talking about? It was the most beautiful sunny day, and there wasn't a cloud in sight. Jasmine must have been thinking exactly the same, because she was frowning. "Excuse me, but how do you know it'll snow?" she asked.

Fairy G chuckled. "That's the advantage of being a fairy godmother," she said. "We can have snow whenever we need it...and we'll need lots of it tomorrow!" And, still chuckling, she led us into Emerald Castle.

Chapter Three

All the way up the stairs I was imagining what Daffodil Room would look like, but when Fairy G opened the door I had SUCH a surprise. It was very light and pretty, and the eight little beds looked really cosy. Our trunks were already there, and I wondered if Fairy G had floated them up the stairs by magic.

"We've put you two together at the end," Fairy G said. "Unpack your things, and when you hear the bell come downstairs for tea.

The dining hall's easy to find; you'll hear the noise!" And with a last wink she was gone.

Jasmine grinned at me. "She's nice," she said. "Hey! What was that about minus tiara points?"

"Mum told me that we get tiara points for being good, and minus ones for being bad," I sighed.

"I think it's going to be all right here." My new friend opened her trunk, and began throwing clothes into her chest of drawers. "I mean, a Snow Sculpture Competition sounds great. And what was that you were saying about a masked ball? FABULOUS!"

"Actually," said an incredibly snooty voice, "it's a Midnight Masquerade. You're the new girls, aren't you?"

We looked up, and there in the doorway were two princesses who just HAD to be twins.

"I'm Princess Diamonde," said the first one, "and this is my sister, Princess Gruella. And WE are going to win the competition."

"That's right." The other sister, Gruella, sounded almost as snooty. "Mummy's promised us we'll win! And guess what – the winners are going to the Midnight Masquerade in a sleigh pulled by the most darling husky dogs! When the ice dancing starts we'll be first on the ice, and the princes will all want to dance with us—"

"Shh!" Diamonde stuck a sharp elbow into Gruella's side. Jasmine jumped up from her unpacking, her eyes shining.

"Did you say husky dogs? Pulling a sleigh? Oh!" She looked round at me. "Wouldn't that be GLORIOUS? Hey, Emma – we REALLY have to win!"

"But I told you." Diamonde glared at Jasmine. "WE'RE going to win. Besides, you're new here. You don't know anything. I bet you can't even skate."

Jasmine glared back. "Actually, I can skate very well."

"Huh!" Diamonde stuck her nose in the air. "We'll see about that. Come along, Gruella." And the two of them linked arms and stomped off.

"Wow," Jasmine said. "Do you think ALL the other princesses will be like those two?"

"I do hope not," I said. I was feeling wobbly again, and wishing I was safely back at home.

There was the sound of a bell ringing, and Jasmine grabbed my hand. "That'll be the tea bell. Let's go and see what horrors are downstairs." She gave me a questioning look. "Are you OK?"

"I think so." I did my best to smile at her, and she gave my hand a squeeze.

"Friends for ever," she said, and I felt a little bit better.

We hurried down the stairs, and saw LOADS of princesses queuing in the corridor. A really pretty girl stopped as soon as she saw us.

"Hi!" she said. "I'm Millie. Are you Emma and Jasmine? You're going to be in Daffodil Room, aren't you? We've been LONGING to meet you. Come on – Leah's saving you places!" And she led us into the dining hall. When we reached our table she pointed at a girl with glasses. "That's Leah. And the girl next to her is Rachel – and that's Amelia, and that's Ruby, and the girl on the end is Zoe." She smiled at me

and Jasmine. "We'll look after you – we promise."

Jasmine didn't smile back. "Are those twins friends of yours?"

"Oh, goodness me," Millie said. "Erm...not exactly."

"We do try hard to be nice to them," Zoe explained, "but they're really mean most of the time."

"Phew." Jasmine sat down, looking much more cheerful, and I sat down beside her. "Emma and I made a pact that we'd stick together, and only be friends with the nicest princesses." She looked round at Millie and the others. "We'd love to be friends with you, wouldn't we, Emma?"

I nodded, and two minutes later we were all chatting as if we'd known each other for ever.

*

Once tea was over, Zoe and Millie showed us round Emerald Castle.

"Did you know there's a Snow Sculpture Competition tomorrow?" Zoe asked as we came back down the stairs.

Jasmine made a face. "The twins told us they're going to win," she said.

Millie snorted. "They always think they'll win. Don't take any notice of them. We thought Daffodil Room could work as a team. Would that be all right with you?"

Of course we said it was, and Millie and Zoe hurried us away to

44

the recreation room. The others had been drawing pictures for the sculpture, and they asked Jasmine and me to choose the one we liked best.

We looked, and I felt really mean, because I didn't terribly like any of them. There was a flying dragon, and a jumping dog, and a bunch of flowers, and I couldn't see how they could be made out of snow.

"Erm..." I said at last. "What about a snow castle? With lots of turrets, like a fairy palace?"

Jasmine cheered, and Ruby clapped her hands. "That would be SO much better!"

Rachel and Leah grinned at me.

"Fantastic!" they said.

Amelia patted me on the back. "I'm SO pleased you're in Daffodil Room!"

I could feel myself blushing. "Thanks," I said, and I suddenly noticed my wobbly feeling had vanished away.

Chapter Four

I'd never slept in a dormitory before, but Daffodil Room was so comfortable I went to sleep as soon as my head touched the pillow. Jasmine had to shake me awake the next morning.

"DO LOOK!" she said. "Come and see! Everywhere's covered in snow!"

I leapt out of bed and ran to the
window – and she was quite right!
It was SO pretty; even the beach
was thickly covered.

"That's REAL magic," I breathed.

Ruby nodded. "Fairy G's amazing," she said.

I got dressed as quickly as I could, and all eight of us dashed down the stairs.

Fairy G was waiting in the dining hall, and she made us eat a proper breakfast even though we were dying to get started on our magical castle.

"You'll be building your sculptures on the beach," she told us. "The snow's thickest there – but watch out for hidden rocks! And don't forget to wear your gloves and boots."

We promised we would, and

hurried outside. Soon the beach was filled with princesses digging and patting and smoothing the snow...but I couldn't see the twins anywhere.

"No, and I don't want to,"

Jasmine said when I asked her if she'd seen them on the beach. "I last saw them hanging round the front entrance to the castle – they looked as if they were waiting for something."

"They told me their mother was sending them a parcel." Rachel sighed. "Probably even MORE wonderful dresses."

"Oh," I said. I quickly forgot about them because our snow castle was beginning to look REALLY special.

Fairy G came stomping through the snow at break time to call us inside for hot chocolate and biscuits. I still hadn't seen the twins, but when we came back out we couldn't miss them...they were standing by the most BEAUTIFUL snow sculpture of a dancing horse.

"WOW!" Jasmine breathed. "That's STUNNING!" Then she looked puzzled. "But you weren't here before break, were you?"

"We decided to surprise you," Diamonde said smugly. "And we work very quickly, don't we, Gruella?"

Gruella nodded. "Mummy sent us a—"

"SHH!" Diamonde hissed before giving us another superior smile. "Hadn't you better get back to your weedy little castle?"

As we walked away Amelia was frowning. "They can't have made that whole horse while we were inside, can they?"

I didn't answer. There had been some strange tracks in the snow beside Diamonde and Gruella's sculpture; they reminded me of something, but I couldn't quite think what...

Chapter Five

We went on working on our castle, and we'd just about finished when we saw Fairy G marching along the beach.

"Well done, all of you! Well done!" Her booming voice echoed as she stopped to look at each sculpture in turn. "Excellent work! A snow dolphin, a dog,

a sailing ship, a castle, a..." She
stopped, and stared at the twins'
dancing horse. "Well I never!"

Diamonde curtsied. "Do you
like it, Fairy G? We did our
very best."

"H'mph. Very professional," Fairy G told her, but it was odd. She didn't sound at all enthusiastic. "Very splendid indeed."

"So have we won?" Gruella asked.

Fairy G shook her head. "Not unless your horse is still here after lunch, Gruella. That's when Queen Gwendoline is coming to admire the winning sculpture."

Diamonde suddenly looked anxious. "But all the snow will have melted by then!" She squinted up at the sun overhead.

Fairy G raised an eyebrow. "Are you suggesting my magic snow won't last, Diamonde? It'll be here until well after the Midnight Masquerade – you wait and see!"

As she stomped away I saw Diamonde and Gruella's faces – and they looked as if they were about to burst into tears.

"It'll NEVER last until after lunch," Gruella wailed. "Look! It's melting already!" And she pointed at the snow horse.

She was quite right. The ears were already drooping, and the head was beginning to sag. I looked at our snow castle, and the other snow sculptures arranged along the beach – and

it was WEIRD! Ours were just as
fresh and crisp as when we'd first
made them. I turned back to stare
at the twins' horse, and as I did so
the head fell off with a soft *flump!*
into the snow beneath.

"OH!" I gasped. "Oh no! That's terrible! Can I help you?" I bent down to scoop up some snow from a pile nearby – and Diamonde jumped forward.

"Dn't touch it!" she said shrilly. "No! Don't!"

But she was too late. I'd seen what was hidden beneath the snow...a sledge. And I knew at once what the track marks were. Someone had dragged the sledge over the snow, and I could guess what had been on it.

"We thought it might be fun to go sledging later," Diamonde said, but it was obvious she was trying to make up an excuse. Gruella didn't even try.

"PLEASE don't tell!" she begged me. "Please! Fairy G will be FURIOUS if she knows we didn't make the horse!"

I hesitated. A Perfect Princess

Never Tells Tales. "I won't tell,"
I said.

Jasmine appeared beside me.
"Emma doesn't need to tell," she
pointed out. "Your horse is made
of a different sort of snow..."

Diamonde stamped her foot. "I
KNOW!" she shouted. "I KNOW!
And when I see Mummy I'm going
to say..." her voice died away.

"You'll say what, exactly,
Diamonde?"

We swung round, and I saw
Fairy G standing behind us, her
arms folded. She was almost
twice her usual size, and she
didn't look kind and friendly any

more. She looked SCARY.

Diamonde gulped. "I...I didn't hear you coming, Fairy G."

Fairy G gave a grim smile. "I'm a fairy, Diamonde. But what were you going to say?"

Diamonde opened and shut her mouth, then burst into angry tears. "I only did it because I wanted to win," she wailed.

"That," Fairy G said coldly, "is the worst excuse I've ever heard. Go back to Emerald Castle, and report yourselves to Queen Gwendoline AT ONCE."

As the twins trailed away across the snow their horse collapsed completely, and was nothing more than a puddle of water. Jasmine looked at Fairy G with an awestruck expression on her face.

"WOW!" she said. "Emma's mum said we should watch out for you, and now I know why!"

For a second I thought Fairy G was going to be cross, but I was wrong. She burst into peals of laughter, and patted Jasmine on the back.

"Never underestimate the power of magic!" she said. "Now, finish your castle." She winked at us all. "The winning entry must be totally perfect when Queen Gwendoline comes to see it!"

We stared at Fairy G, and then at each other.

"You mean...you mean, we've WON?" Ruby asked breathlessly.

"You certainly have." Fairy G beamed at us. "Look at all those turrets! It's wonderful."

For a moment we were too stunned to say anything, and then we whooped with delight...and we spent the rest of the day in a rosy glow of excitement.

We were going to go to the Midnight Masquerade in a sleigh ...and it was going to be pulled by husky dogs!

Chapter Six

That night we just couldn't stop talking.

"It's so lovely you and Jasmine are here, Emma," Zoe said as she brushed her hair. "If it hadn't been for your idea we'd never have won the competition."

Rachel nodded. "That's right. We couldn't have done it without you."

"What are you going to wear?" Amelia wanted to know, and we described our dresses, and our shoes, and then we asked Amelia what she was going to wear, and Leah and the others... until finally Fairy G came stomping up the stairs.

"Time to go to sleep!" she said firmly. "We don't want any sleepy heads tomorrow morning. Queen Gwendoline has decided you can have extra ice dancing classes every day between now and the Midnight Masquerade!"

"Wow," Jasmine said as she snuggled into her pillows. "This is the best place ever. I can't think why I made such a fuss about coming here..."

And I quite agreed with her.

Emerald Castle was truly amazing...

And I'm so, so, SO glad you're here too!

Hey – I'm Princess Jasmine!
How are you? Did Princess Emma
tell you the amazing news? We won the
Snow Sculpture Competition, so we're
going to go to the Midnight Masquerade
in a sleigh pulled by huskies!
Isn't that SO fabulous?
And the Midnight Masquerade will
be wonderful too – as long as the
horrible twins don't spoil it...

Chapter One

I woke up very early on the day of the Midnight Masquerade, and found my friends in Daffodil Room were already awake. Amelia said she'd been dreaming of sleigh rides, and Leah laughed.

"Did you dream you stayed on, or fell off?" she asked.

"I dreamt the sleigh went up

among the stars," Amelia said
dreamily. "It was SO romantic."

Emma looked anxious. "You
don't think the sleigh will really
fly, do you?"

Zoe shook her head. "Not unless the huskies have grown wings. When are we allowed to get ready?"

"Fairy G said we were to have a quiet day with a nap after lunch, and to start getting ready after tea," Ruby told her. "I don't think I'll ever be able to sleep, though."

I thought exactly the same, but later on that day we all started yawning. I don't know if Fairy G had scattered sleepy dust over our soup at lunchtime, but not one of us complained when she sent us upstairs. As soon as we lay down on our beds we were fast asleep, and we didn't wake up until the bell went for tea.

"Wow!" I said as I sat up and stretched. "Not long now!"

Millie grinned at me. "Are you feeling nervous? I am. What do we do if none of the princes ask us to dance?"

"We dance with each other." I hopped out of bed, and put my shoes on. "Are we taking our ice skates in the sleigh with us?"

Rachel rolled her eyes, and pretended to sigh at me. "I knew you weren't listening yesterday. Fairy G said Queen Gwendoline's going to take all the skates with her in her coach, and they'll be waiting for us in the cloakroom when we arrive. We were meant to put them in the basket last night."

"Oops," I said. "I forgot. Will that mean loads of minus tiara points, do you think?"

"It's all right," Emma said. "I put yours in with mine."

Emma is just the very best friend
anyone could have. I gave her
a massive hug, and we hurried
down the stairs for tea. Fairy G
came to find us just as we were
finishing, and told us the sleigh

would be waiting for us outside the school front door at six o'clock...and we looked at each other with shining eyes.

"That's SO exciting," Rachel said. "I can't wait."

Fairy G smiled at us. "You'd better run upstairs and change. Don't forget to wear your warmest cloaks! It'll be cold on the sleigh." She patted my arm. "Queen Gwendoline says one of the princes is a skating champion, Jasmine – he'll be a good partner for you. Your skating is excellent!"

As we got up from the table Diamonde glared at me. "I'M a champion skater," she said. "I bet I'm LOADS better than you are."

"Mummy says we're the best at everything," Gruella agreed. "And WE should have won the sculpture competition, not you."

I opened my mouth to tell her she was SO wrong, but Emma grabbed my hand and pulled me away.

"Don't take any notice of them," she whispered.

Millie nodded. "They're cross because they got masses of minus tiara points for cheating."

"AND they've got to go to the Starlit Ballroom early, so they can help Queen Gwendoline," Ruby pointed out.

"Don't let's worry about them," Zoe said. "Let's go and get ready!"

We hurried up the stairs to Daffodil room. Our beautiful ball dresses were hanging up waiting for us, and it was SO exciting to put them on at last.

"WOW!" I said as I looked round at the others. "You look really FABULOUS!"

"You do too, Jasmine," Emma said with a smile.

Amelia did a twirl in front of the mirror. "When do we get our masks?" she asked.

"When we get there." Leah winked at me. "Maybe we won't recognise each other!"

That made me laugh, and I was still laughing as we hurried down the stairs to collect our warm winter cloaks and muffs. As soon as we were wrapped up we made our way to the front hall...and the door swung open.

Chapter Two

"Ohhhhhh..." we gasped. Outside the front door was the most glorious silver sleigh heaped with velvet cushions and the softest rugs. It was pulled by eight snow-white husky dogs, and each dog had a bell on its collar – and as they turned to look at us the bells made the sweetest tinkling sound.

The driver wore a thick white woollen cloak, and he bowed as we stood and stared.

"Welcome, Your Highnesses," he said. "Please step into my sleigh!"

I could hardly breathe as I climbed into my seat, and Emma settled herself beside me. A small page hurried forward to tuck the rugs over our knees, and to arrange the cushions behind our backs.

"I feel like a queen!" Rachel whispered, and Zoe smiled her widest smile.

"Me too," she said.

"Are we ready?" the driver asked, and when we said we were he cracked his whip, and the huskies began to run.

What was it like?

I don't think I've got enough

words to tell you. It was exactly like flying, and the snow flew up in sparkling flurries around us as we zoomed along. The little page sat at the back of the sleigh

and played a concertina, and sometimes the tunes were so happy they made us laugh, and sometimes they were so sad I got a terrible lump in my throat.

We arrived with a wonderful WHOOOOSH! in front of the Starlit Ballroom, and for a long moment none of us wanted to move. The huskies sat down and wagged their tails...and at last we climbed out.

"Thank you!" we said. "Thank you so, SO much!"

"That was MAGIC," Emma added, and the driver grinned at her.

"I'm glad you enjoyed your ride," he said. "Perhaps I'll see you again."

"See us again?" We looked at him in astonishment.

"I'll be taking the winners of the dancing competition back to Emerald Castle," the driver told us. Then he turned and whistled to his dogs. "Remember – enjoy the Midnight Masquerade!"

We pulled our cloaks around us, and waved goodbye. Then, taking a deep breath, we walked over the snow to the wide open doors.

As soon as we were inside we realised why it was called

the Starlit Ballroom. It wasn't a proper building; it was a huge tent, and the canvas ceiling was covered with twinkling stars set in a dark blue sky. The floor was shining ice, and the stars were reflected as if it was a mirror.

There were silver chairs and tables arranged round the dance floor, and more stars glittered and shone on the walls behind them. Wreaths of silver roses and glistening frosted ivy were wound round the tent poles, and crystal candelabras sparkled up above our heads.

It's not often I can't think of anything to say, but I really was speechless. I gazed and gazed, until Millie pulled at my arm. "Come on," she said. "We've got to put our cloaks away, and find our skates...and Queen Gwendoline's waiting to give us our masks."

I followed her, and found the rest of Daffodil Room hanging their cloaks on a row of hooks in a side room that led off the main tent. Diamonde and Gruella were there too, and to my amazement they looked really cheerful.

"You'll find your skates over there on the shelves." Diamonde sounded very pleased with herself. "Oh, except for yours, Jasmine. I saw you coming, so I got them down for you."

Queen Gwendoline swept into the room, and heard what Diamonde was saying. "That's kind of you, Diamonde," she said encouragingly. "I'm delighted to see you being so helpful. It appears you have both learnt your lesson, so you may join the other princesses, and take part in the ball."

Diamonde sank into a curtsey.

"Thank you, Your Majesty."

"Thank you so much." Gruella curtsied too.

"Excellent!" Queen Gwendoline turned to us. "Ah! Daffodil Room! Here are your masks, my dears, and I hope you have a wonderful evening."

Chapter Three

The masks were SO pretty! They were decorated with butterflies and silver roses, and as we held them in front of our faces we couldn't help smiling to see how different we looked.

"Aren't you going to put your skates on?" Diamonde asked. "The others will be here soon, and

it'll get really crowded. Besides – "
she patted her curls – "the princes
will arrive any minute, and we
must be ready for them."

I'd almost forgotten that the
princes from the Princes' Academy
were going to be at the ball, but

I wasn't surprised that Diamonde went all fluttery. I picked up my boots and put them on. They felt a bit odd, but I tied up my laces and walked over to the dance floor. A moment later I was gliding on the ice, and at first it felt wonderful.

Emma, Ruby, Zoe and the others came to join me, and we held hands and swung each other round, even though the music hadn't started. It should have been fun, but my feet were feeling more and more uncomfortable. My toes felt really cramped, and my heels were rubbing. I was glad when there was a fanfare of trumpets and we had to stop. Queen Gwendoline came sailing past us followed by Fairy G, and I couldn't help smiling. They were holding masks in front of their faces, but it was SO obvious who they were – especially Fairy G.

"Dear princesses," our head teacher said, as she took her place on a glittering throne at the far end of the tent. "I wish you all the most wonderful evening. The princes have just arrived, and the dancing will begin very shortly, but first I have something

to tell you all. There will be a dance competition later this evening, and the winners will go home to Emerald Castle on the silver sleigh!"

There was a ripple of applause, and I saw Diamonde and Gruella nudge each other.

"And now," Queen Gwendoline went on, "please welcome King Gustav and the princes from the Princes' Academy!"

A tall king skated gracefully towards Queen Gwendoline, spun round twice, and soared into the air before landing at her feet with a low bow.

"That's one of the teachers from the Princes' Academy," Leah whispered in my ear.

I was about to say I thought he was brilliant at skating, but just then the princes came hurrying into the ballroom. They were carrying their skates, and there was a buzz of conversation as they sat down and put them on. A moment later they were up and on the ice, and the musicians began to play the most glorious waltz tune ever. My feet began to twitch, and I just LONGED to dance...and I saw a prince wearing a silver cat mask gliding towards me.

"Would you care to be my partner?" he asked, and I curtsied before giving him my hand. I held my mask up with the other hand, and we swirled away...and for at least five minutes I completely forgot my aching feet. He was

SUCH a good skater, and he was funny as well. He kept making silly jokes, and trying to make me laugh so he could see my face. (If I'm really truthful, I did peep over the top just once...or maybe twice.)

Then the music changed, and got faster and faster. I've always adored skating, and it was fabulous to be dancing with someone so good. When the prince said, "Shall we try a triple spin?", I said yes, and he grinned at me.

"Hang on tight, then," he said, and began to whizz me round – and suddenly my feet felt SO painful that I wobbled, and let go of his hands. He flew one way, and I flew the other...right into the middle of the musicians.

Chapter Four

There was a simply dreadful tooting banging crashing noise, and the music stopped.

"Princess Jasmine!" Queen Gwendoline came sailing towards me looking absolutely FURIOUS. "What WERE you thinking? I understood from Fairy G that you were one of our best skaters!

NOBODY should attempt a triple spin if they don't know what they're doing!"

I staggered to my feet. "I'm so sorry, Your Majesty," I said. "It was an accident..."

"Go and sit down," Queen Gwendoline snapped. "You are not to dance any more. You can consider yourself fortunate that I'm not sending you straight back to Emerald Castle!"

"Yes, Your Majesty." I wanted to explain what had happened, but I knew it would sound as if I was just trying to make excuses. As I limped away I saw Diamonde rush forward to talk to the prince in the cat mask. He was dusting himself down, and rubbing his elbows.

"Excuse me," Diamonde said, and she was fluttering her eyelashes quite dreadfully. "You should never have danced with Jasmine." She gave a silly little snigger. "It's ME that's the champion skater." She grabbed his hand and pulled him onto the ice, then began to show off with all kinds of twirls and pirouettes. I took myself into the little side room, where I collapsed onto a bench.

"Oh, my poor feet!" I groaned. I dragged off my boots, and dumped them on the bench beside me. One of them fell over the edge, and as I picked it up I wondered again why it had felt so tight. "Maybe my feet have grown," I thought, and put my hand inside – and found the toes were stuffed with crumpled up sheets of paper!

"No wonder my feet were so uncomfortable!" I pulled the paper out. "Diamonde must have put it in there!" There was more paper in my other boot, and I saw it was a list of names. To my surprise it

was written in Queen Gwendoline's
handwriting. I was staring at it so
hard I didn't notice Emma had
come to stand beside me.

"Are you OK?" she asked, and I jumped. "We're all so worried about you. Why don't you come and sit by the ice rink? We can talk to you there, even if you're not allowed to dance."

I put the bits of paper into my pocket, and pulled my skating boots back on. "Yes," I said slowly. My mind was racing. Was there anything I could do, without being a horrible telltale? I couldn't think of any ideas, so I went to sit at one of the pretty tables on the edge of the ice. Emma sat with me for a little while, but a tall prince wearing a bird mask soon whisked her away, and I was left on my own. Diamonde gave me the snootiest look as she danced past with Gruella, but I pretended not to notice.

"Hello, Jasmine." It was the prince in the cat mask. He was standing behind me in the shadows, and I did just wonder if he was hiding from Diamonde.

"That was a horrible tumble you took. Why did you wobble? You're much too good a skater to make a mistake like that."

I smiled at him. "That's nice of you. I'm very sorry I made you fall over – I saw you rubbing your elbows."

He laughed. "No problem. I'm always falling over. Will you dance with me again?"

I was about to explain that I wasn't allowed to, when Queen Gwendoline stood up and clapped her hands for silence.

"Princesses and princes," she said. "King Gustav and I have

decided to hold the dancing competition before supper, rather than later when you may be tired. I will read out your names, and King Gustav will announce the name of the prince who will partner you. Diamonde, my dear – could you fetch me the lists? I gave them to you to look after when you were being so very helpful earlier on this evening."

There was a sudden silence.

"Erm...yes, of course, Your Majesty." Diamonde's voice sounded strange. "Erm...I think Gruella had them last. Didn't you, Gruella?"

There was an outraged squeak from Gruella. "I SO didn't," she said indignantly. "YOU had them, Diamonde!"

Diamonde turned on her twin, and glared at her. "No I didn't! YOU did!"

"Don't go blaming me!" Gruella folded her arms, and glared back at Diamonde. "You said you wanted some paper so I gave them to you. And I know what you did with them, too. You crumpled them up and stuffed them in Jasmine's boots!"

"WHAT WAS THAT?" Fairy G has the loudest voice in the whole wide world when she's angry. She also grows enormous, and looks REALLY scary. I wasn't a bit surprised when Diamonde tried to hide behind Gruella.

"I...I didn't know Gruella had given me the lists," she quavered.

"I...I thought it was just scrap paper..."

"NEVER MIND THE LISTS!" Fairy G boomed. "What was that about putting paper in Jasmine's boots?" She swung round and looked straight at me. "WAS there

anything in your boots, Jasmine?"

When Fairy G is angry you answer her questions as quickly as you can. I put my hand in my pocket, and held out the crumpled lists. Fairy G took them, and gave the twins a VERY cold look.

"What exactly did you hope to achieve by this?" she asked, and Diamonde burst into tears.

"I was only playing a little joke," she sobbed. "I thought it would make Jasmine laugh. I didn't mean to be nasty..."

Gruella looked at her twin in surprise. "Yes, you did. You wanted to stop Jasmine being the best skater. You said so!"

Diamonde stopped crying so suddenly it was obvious she'd been pretending. "Don't tell fibs!" she shouted, but before she could say anything else Fairy G took her by one arm and Gruella by the other.

"I think we'll have a little talk in the cloakroom," she said grimly, and marched them away.

As they disappeared the prince standing behind me stepped forward, and bowed to our head teacher.

"Your Majesty," he said, "might I suggest that Princess Jasmine fell because her boots were hurting her? If you would permit it, I would like to show you that she is, in fact, the most wonderful dancer." And before Queen Gwendoline could say yes or no, he led me onto the ice. "Ready?" he asked, and his eyes were twinkling behind his mask. "Let's show them!"

The musicians began to play a wild polka, and off we went.

We spun and we twirled and we flew round and round, and when at last the music stopped every single prince and princess jumped up and cheered. Queen Gwendoline clapped harder than anyone, and

she actually came over and gave me a hug. King Gustav patted me on the back.

"Excellent!" he said. "Princess Jasmine – you and Prince Dudley make a splendid couple!"

*

Boom! Boom! Boom!

We'd had the most DELICIOUS supper, and, before we knew it, there was the sound of a clock

striking twelve. Fairy G stood up
and waved her wand. Hundreds of
tiny silver birds flew round and
round the Starlit Ballroom, and as
they flew they twittered and sang

until at last they faded away.

"Midnight!" Fairy G announced, and we took off our masks...and guess what?

Prince Dudley wasn't exactly the most handsome prince I'd ever seen, but he had MUCH the nicest face. He gave me a huge grin.

"Nice to meet you, Princess Jasmine," he said, and then he bowed, and kissed my hand.

Chapter Six

The ride home on the sleigh
was just as magical as the first
time. The page played gentle
lullabies, so I very nearly went
to sleep...except we had so
much to talk about. When we
got out we were allowed to pat
the huskies, and they had the
softest ears.

As we got into bed Ruby yawned, and smiled at the rest of us. "Aren't we the luckiest princesses ever?" she said. "Eight wonderful

friends, and we're all in Daffodil Room together."

"That's right," Zoe agreed, but I knew Ruby was wrong.

She should have said NINE wonderful friends...because you're here too, and I'm SO pleased you are.

Goodnight!

Don't miss **Tiara** *The* *Club* *website at:*

www.tiaraclub.co.uk

Keep up to date with the latest
Tiara Club books and meet all
your favourite princesses!

There is SO much to see and do,
including games and activities. You can
even become an exclusive member of the
Tiara Club Princess Academy.

PLUS, there's exciting
competitions with
WONDERFUL prizes!

Be a Perfect Princess – check it out today!

Look out for

The Tiara Club

at Diamond Turrets

Coming soon!

Here's a taster of Princess Mia and the Magical Koala...

Hi there - and isn't it SO exciting? We're at Diamond Turrets at last - and all of us in Tulip Room are really REALLY pleased you're here too. Oh! I'm so silly! I haven't told you who I am! I'm Princess Mia, and I share Tulip Room with Bethany, Caitlin, Lindsey, Abigail and Rebecca - we've been best friends for ever. Do you love animals? I do, and that's why I'm SO pleased to be here...

I've always loved animals. My mum and dad get SO cross with me, because I'm always smuggling lost kittens or hedgehogs or frogs into my bedroom. Once I rescued a nest of baby mice, and when my mum found them in my wardrobe she screamed so loudly my dad sent six soldiers running to save her! My aunt, Queen Elisabetta, travels all the time and she adores the animals she meets; it's weird that my mum is always scared. She and Aunt Elisabetta are sisters, after all – I don't know why they're so different.

So you'll understand why I just

couldn't wait to get to Diamond Turrets. My dad told me that the head teacher, King Percy, thinks princesses should know how to look after animals as well as people. "It'll be very good for you, Mia," my dad went on, "you'll learn a lot. There's a wildlife park as well as the home farm – and I believe there's a place where people can board their pets when they're away on holiday."

"Can I take Whiskers with me?" I asked hopefully, but my dad shook his head.

"There'll be plenty of animals at Diamond Turrets," he said firmly.

"And cats don't like travelling if they're not used to it."

I knew my dad was right, so I didn't try to argue. I rushed upstairs to make sure I had everything I needed in my trunk. It all looked fine, and I zoomed back down to the stables. I absolutely had to say goodbye to every single one of the ponies and the horses, and the kitten in the hayloft, and the stable boy's dog...

"Mia!" My dad was sounding cross, so I hurried back. Our travelling coach was in the courtyard, and my trunks were piled up on the roof. I suddenly realised I must have been much, MUCH longer than I meant to be.

"Ooops," I said as I climbed inside. "I'm really sorry!"

My dad sighed heavily. "Maybe you'll learn to behave more like a Perfect Princess this term," he said. "Do try and stop rushing everywhere, Mia!"

I promised, and kissed him goodbye, and then my mum came sailing out carrying a basket.

"REALLY, Mia!" She frowned at me, which I didn't think was very nice of her. After all, I was just about to go off to school.

"You'd forgotten your hairbrush, your toothbrush, your pyjamas AND your best tiara! What WERE you thinking of?"

"Animals," my dad said, but there was a twinkle in his eye so I knew he wasn't cross any more. "Let's hope King Percy and Lady Whitstable-Kent can cope with you. I know we can't!"

"Who's Lady...what did you say?" I asked.

"Lady Whitstable-Kent," my dad explained. "She looks after everything. I'm sure you'll like her."

And then my mum put the

basket beside me, and gave me a hug...and she and my dad stood waving as the coach trundled out of the courtyard. I was on my way to Diamond Turrets at last!

Emerald Castle had been a proper castle on a hill above the sea, and I'd thought Diamond Turrets would be the same – but it wasn't at all. There was a long driveway up through a country park, and I got wildly excited because I thought I saw a lion, but Frank, the footman, said it was only a cow. Then we passed some farm buildings, and finally we drove up in front of a low white building covered in pink roses with little sparkly turrets at either end. The front door was wide open, but I couldn't see any sign of any other princesses. In fact, the whole place looked deserted.

~ Want to read more? ~
Princess Mia and the Magical Koala is published in 2009

The Tiara Club books are priced at £3.99. *Butterfly Ball, Christmas Wonderland, Princess Parade, Emerald Ball* and *Midnight Masquerade* are priced at £5.99. The Tiara Club books are available from all good bookshops, or can be ordered direct from the publisher:
Orchard Books, PO BOX 29, Douglas IM99 1BQ.
Credit card orders please telephone 01624 836000 or fax 01624 837033 or visit our website: www.orchardbooks.co.uk or e-mail: bookshop@enterprise.net for details.

To order please quote title, author and ISBN and your full name and address.
Cheques and postal orders should be made payable to 'Bookpost plc.'
Postage and packing is FREE within the UK
(overseas customers should add £2.00 per book).
Prices and availability are subject to change.